D1093764

OCT 0 1 2021

NO LONGER PROPERTY OF
SEATTLE PUBLIC LIBRARY

To my sister

About This Book

The illustrations for this book were done in watercolor on eggshell-textured paper. This book was designed by Véronique Lefèvre Sweet. The production was supervised by Erika Schwartz, and the production editor was Marisa Finkelstein. The text was set in Adobe Garamond Pro Regular, and the display type is Wanderlust Letters Pro Regular.

Copyright © 2020 by Soosh/Vskafandre Inc. • Cover illustration copyright © 2020 by Soosh/Vskafandre Inc. Cover design by Véronique Lefèvre Sweet. • Cover copyright © 2020 by Hachette Book Group, Inc. • Hachette Book Group supports the right to free expression and the value of copyright. The purpose of copyright is to encourage writers and artists to produce the creative works that enrich our culture. • The scanning, uploading, and distribution of this book without permission is a theft of the author's intellectual property. If you would like permission to use material from the book (other than for review purposes), please contact permissions@hbgusa.com. Thank you for your support of the author's rights. • Little, Brown and Company • Hachette Book Group • 1290 Avenue of the Americas, New York, NY 10104 • Visit us at LBYR.com • First Edition: April 2020 • Little, Brown and Company is a division of Hachette Book Group, Inc. • The Little, Brown name and logo are trademarks of Hachette Book Group, Inc. • The publisher is not responsible for websites (or their content) that are not owned by the publisher. • Library of Congress Cataloging-in-Publication Data • Names: Soosh, author, illustrator. • Title: Mermaid and me / written and illustrated by Soosh. • Description: First edition. | New York: Little, Brown and Company, 2020. | Audience: Ages 4–8. | Summary: A girl and a mermaid become best friends as they figure out how to enjoy their favorite things together, but when the shore becomes unsafe Mermaid must leave, promising to return. • Identifiers: LCCN 2019031288 | ISBN 9780316426626 (hardcover) | ISBN 9780316426602 (ebook) | ISBN 9780316426657 (ebook) • Subjects: CYAC: Best friends—Fiction. | Friendship—Fiction. | Mermaids—Fiction. | Environmental protection—Fiction. • Classification: LCC PZ7.1.S6774 Mer 2020 | DDC [E]—dc23 • LC record available at https://lccn.loc.gov/2019031288 • ISBNs: 978-0-316-42662-6 (hardcover), 978-0-316-42663-3 (ebook), 978-0-316-42660-2 (ebook), 978-0-316-42664-0 (ebook) • PRINTED IN CHINA • APS • 10 9 8 7 6 5 4 3 2 1

Mermaid
and Me

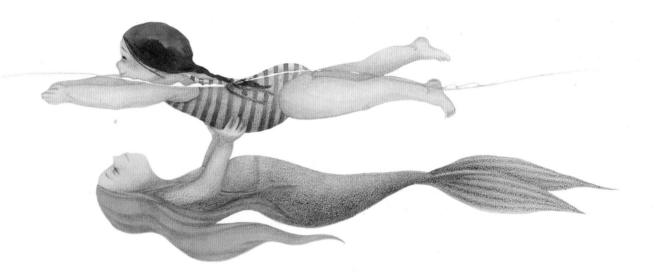

Written and illustrated by SOOSH

L B

Little, Brown and Company
New York • Boston

This is me, the girl wearing
a mermaid tail, in an old class
photo. I really loved mermaids.

I was not a popular girl.
My classmates didn't believe in mermaids.

They would laugh, call me names, and
never ask me to play games.

Sometimes when I felt lonely, I would imagine I saw a mermaid in the water. She seemed so real, but it was only the sunlight playing on the waves.

One day, I was looking at the sea when I saw the top of a head, blue eyes, and a button nose emerge from the water. Then our eyes met.

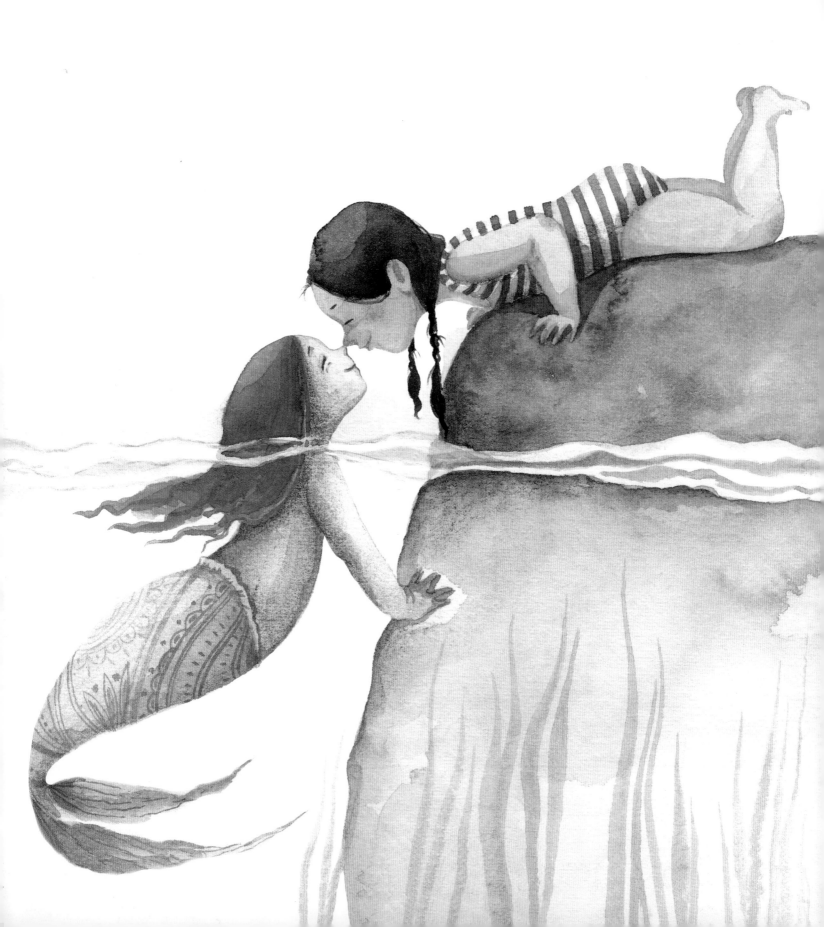

"You are a mermaid!" I exclaimed in delight.

The mermaid shook her head. "No, I am a girl. An underwater girl." She paused. "You know, I like how *mermaid* sounds. You can call me Mermaid. And who are you?"

"I am a girl too," I said. "An aboveground girl!"

We became friends and would spend our time together, learning about each other and having many adventures.

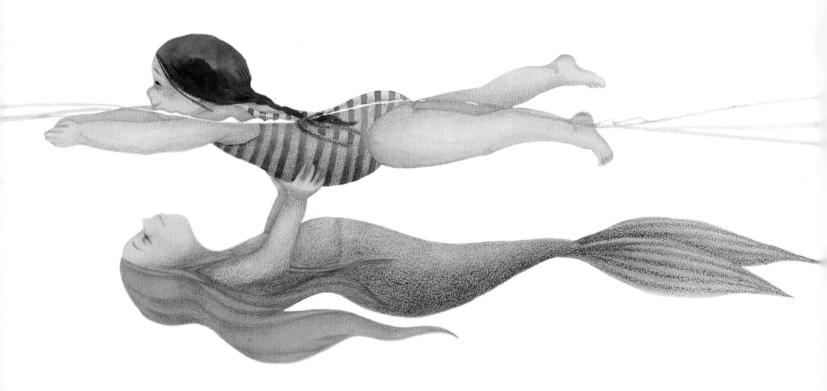

Mermaid invited me to follow her to the bottom of the sea to look for beautiful shells. I shook my head and said, "I wish I could, but I can't swim."

She smiled, splashed with her palms, and said, *"But you will! We will!"*

And when we swam together, she held me gently and promised to never let go.

Once Mermaid and I found a turtle caught
in a piece of plastic and helped set it free.

When our work was done, we watched
the turtle disappear in the waves.

Mermaid was learning so much about my way of life, like how it felt to ride a bicycle with the wind blowing through my hair.

"I have never ridden a bicycle. I don't think I ever will," said Mermaid as she looked at her tail.

I jumped up and clapped my hands. *"But you will! We will!"*

I told my friend that one of my favorite things
to do was have a tea party.

Mermaid sighed and said, "I wish I could go. I have never been to a tea party."

I smiled. *"But you will! We will!"*

That day, we had one of the best tea parties in between our two worlds.

Sometimes we spotted a fisherman. When he wasn't looking, we would dive in and place an old shoe on his hook. The fisherman scratched his head as he fished out one boot after another.

We would hide behind a rock and giggle.

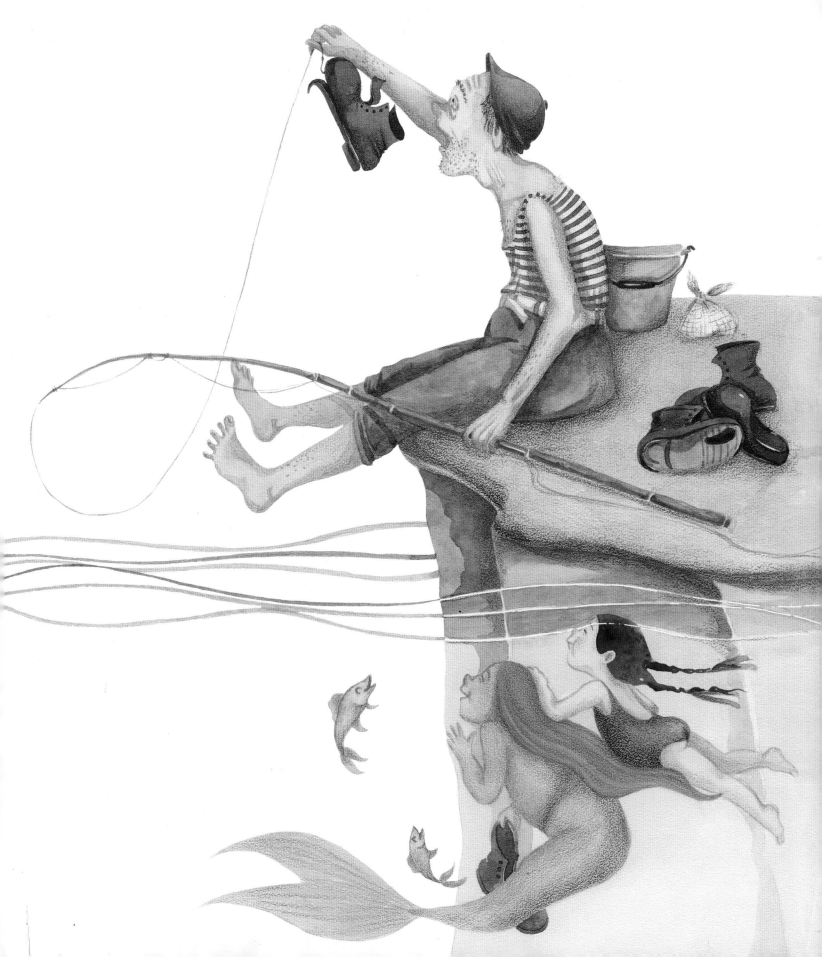

And on hot summer days, we would sit quietly,
dreaming our own dreams together.

One night, there was a big storm. It had
brought all kinds of garbage to the surface.
I couldn't wait till the morning to see if my
friend was safe. I looked and called out for
Mermaid everywhere. Finally, I spotted her.

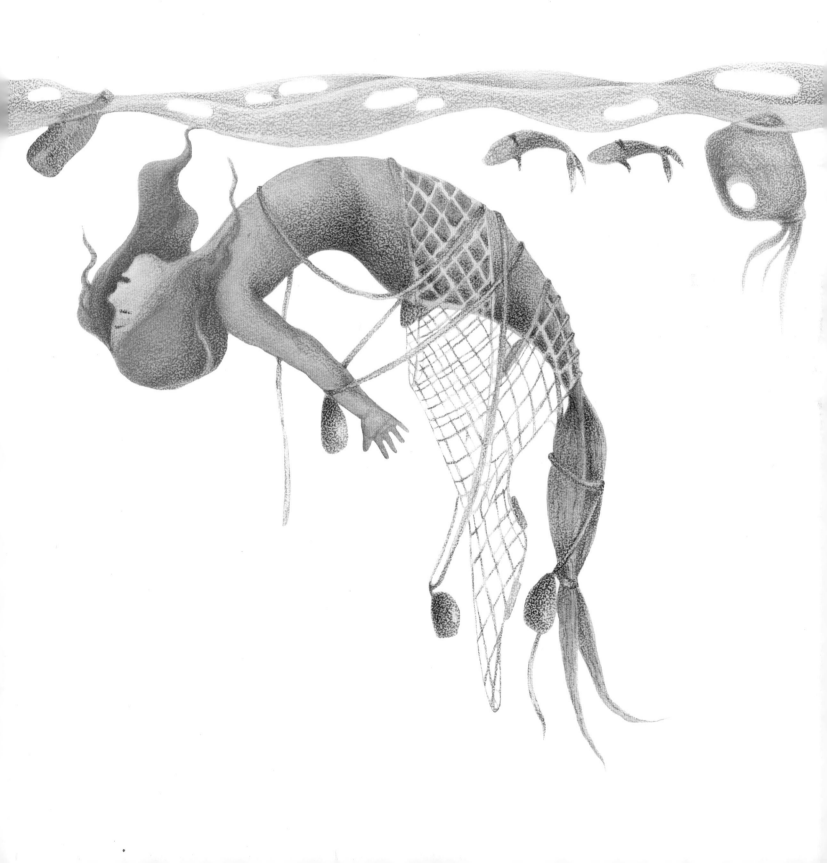

I tried to untangle Mermaid, but the net was too strong. I needed help and saw a few of my classmates on the beach.

"I know you don't believe me, and you think mermaids are fairy tales. But, please, believe me this once!" I cried. "There is a mermaid caught in a net, and she needs our help."

My classmates were silent for a moment. Then they turned to me and said, "Show us the way."

Together we managed to set Mermaid free.

"Thank you, my friends, for saving me," said Mermaid. "But I must leave. It's not safe for me here."

"Will I ever see you again?" I asked, wiping my tears.

"Yes, you will. We will see each other again."

And from that day on, my classmates and I picked up any garbage we found on the shore so that Mermaid could return someday.

I grew up and had a family. And all that time, I hoped to see Mermaid again. . . .

Until one day, I did.

Author's Note

When I decided to participate in an annual #mermaid challenge on Instagram, in May 2018, I didn't know if the series of illustrations about Mermaid and the little girl would ever become a book.

I wanted to tell a story of two different beings who, when you look closer, prove to be so much alike. I wanted to show their story through the eyes of a child, because in our world, adults often get distracted by shapes and colors and other external qualities. And here come children. They help us look past those differences and right into the core of it all, and in that core, everyone and everything is the same. Love is the only true quality of us all.

So, the more I drew and shared, the more feedback and letters I received from people asking to turn the drawings into a picture book. This book became possible not only because of the work of all those amazing people who helped to shape these illustrations into a book, but also because of you, people who carry kindness in their hearts and childhood memories in their souls.

Thank you!

SOOSH